D-BOT SQUAD

Dino Hunter

First published by Allen & Unwin in 2017

Allen & Unwin
83 Alexander Street
Crows Nest NSW 2065
Australia
Phone: (61 2) 8425 0100
Email: info@allenandunwin.com
Web: www.allenandunwin.com

A Cataloguing-in-Publication entry is
available from the National Library of Australia
www.trove.nla.gov.au

ISBN 978 1 76029 597 4

For teaching resources, explore
www.allenandunwin.com/resources/for-teachers

Cover and text design by Sandra Nobes
Set in 16 pt ITC Stone Informal by Sandra Nobes
This book was printed in April 2017 at
McPherson's Printing Group, Australia.

1 3 5 7 9 10 8 6 4 2

macparkbooks.com

MIX
Paper from
responsible sources
FSC
www.fsc.org   FSC® C001695

The paper in this book is FSC® certified.
FSC® promotes environmentally responsible,
socially beneficial and economically viable
management of the world's forests.

D-BOT SQUAD

BOOK 1
Dino Hunter

MAC PARK

Illustrated by JAMES HART

ALLEN&UNWIN
SYDNEY•MELBOURNE•AUCKLAND•LONDON

Chapter One

Hunter Marks ran into class. He was happy! Book Week was here at last.

Hunter loved books. He loved books about dinosaurs the most. He loved anything about dinosaurs!

Hunter sat at his desk and looked around the room. Everyone was dressed up for the Book Week parade. *There are lots of super heroes*, Hunter thought. He looked down at his dinosaur book on his desk. *But I'm a dinosaur hunter!*

Just then, two boys dressed as super heroes came and stood at Hunter's desk.

'What are you?' Super Boy asked.

'You're not dressed up at all,' said Bat Kid. 'You're nothing.'

'**I am so!**' Hunter said. He tapped the book on his desk.

'I'm the dinosaur hunter from this book,' Hunter said. 'I know all about every dino in here. So there!'

'You and your dumb dino thing,' Bat Kid said.

'We're sick of it!' Super Boy added, pushing Hunter's dino-model over.

'Hey!' Hunter cried. 'I made that for the parade. Leave it alone!'

Bat Kid and Super Boy laughed and walked away. Hunter stared after them and kicked the leg of his desk.

Crash!

And leave **me** *alone, too,* he thought.

Hunter picked up his dino-model. He put its head back in place. Then he turned the dino-model around to face him. *How could anyone get sick of dinosaurs?* he thought. *Ahmed and Tom are so weird!*

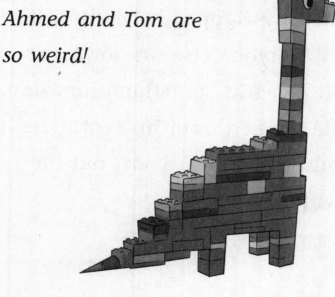

Hunter looked out the window. His mind was busy making lists. Lists of dinosaurs. And lists of dinosaur facts.

Ms Day clapped her hands. But as everyone else sat down, Hunter saw something amazing. He jumped from his seat. 'Miss, miss!' he cried. 'Look, out the window! Hurry!'

Ms Day ran to the window.
'What is it, Hunter?'

'A real dinosaur!' Hunter said,
hopping from foot to foot.
'It flew over the Year 5 and 6
block. Didn't you see it?'

'Oh, Hunter!' said Ms Day
kindly. 'What a story! You can
write about it for me in your
writing book.'

Everyone laughed and Hunter's
face felt hot. 'I really did see it.
It's not a story.' Hunter opened
his dino-book and pointed to
the page.

'It was this one!' he said.

'It was a pterodactyl, and there
was something in its beak.
The pointy thing on its head
is called a crest.'

Pterodactyl
(ter-a-dak-tal)

Legs

Crest

Wings

Teeth

'Stop telling lies,' Bat Kid yelled.

'There are no such things as dinosaurs any more,' Super Boy said. 'And everyone knows it.'

Hunter stamped his foot. **Stomp.** He hit the window with his hands. 'It was out there. I saw it. **It was real.**'

'Everyone sit down now,'
Ms Day said firmly. 'Hunter,
can you take these books back
to the library for me? The walk
will do you good. No dinosaur
hunting along the way. Okay?'

Chapter Two

Hunter stomped into the library with his dino-model and the books. He slammed the books down on the table and looked up at Ms Stegg.

'I know I saw it,' he said. 'It was real!'

'Hello, Hunter,' Ms Stegg said. 'What was real? What did you see?'

Hunter told Ms Stegg the whole story and waited. *Ms Stegg won't laugh*, he thought. *Ms Stegg never laughs at me.*

'Wow!' said Ms Stegg. 'I wish I'd seen that pterodactyl. Do you think it's still out there?'

'I didn't see it again on my way here,' Hunter said. 'But it must be, right? Did you know pteros had four fingers? They lived in caves and trees!'

Ms Stegg smiled. 'Yes, and they liked to live near the sea, too, didn't they?'

Hunter's a dino-whiz!

Their bones were filled with air.

Hunter felt better. *I knew* **she** *would believe me*, he thought.

'Have you seen the dino-cave I made for Book Week yet?' Ms Stegg asked.

'No way! A dino-cave?' Hunter said. 'Where?'

Ms Stegg pointed to the back of the library.

Hunter went to the cave and peered inside. 'Real dinosaurs would have lived in caves just like this. It's awesome.'

Ms Stegg laughed. 'It took me ages to make.'

'There are building blocks in here, too!' Hunter cried.

'Yes, you could build a new dinosaur,' Ms Stegg said.

'I can build one to battle mine,' Hunter said, holding up his dino-model.

'That's the best d-bot I've ever seen,' Ms Stegg said. 'You sure know how to build them, Hunter Marks!'

'D-bot!' Hunter said, smiling.
'What a great name. I do know
everything about dinosaurs.
That's why I'm a dino-hunter
for the book parade.'

'In you go, then,' Ms Stegg said.
'I'll let Ms Day know where you
are.'

Hunter stepped inside the cave
and sank down into a bean
bag.

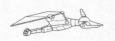

He looked around. *This is the best!* he thought. *Just me, in a dino-cave with my dino-model. No super-hero kids and no noise.*

Hunter rested his back against the wall. As he did, the wall fell away. Hunter tumbled from the cave and the library. He wasn't at school any more.

Woah!

Chapter Three

Hunter stood up and looked around. He was in a big room and he was alone. At the end of the room was a table.

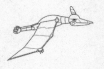

Where am I? thought Hunter.
*And what happened to the cave
in the library?*

A huge screen on the wall
next to the table lit up. Hunter
walked towards it. As he did,
a digital voice began to talk.
'Game starting.'

It's a game! thought Hunter.
*I have to build a d-bot to catch
a ptero. A ptero just like the one
I saw at school.*

A button on the touch screen
began to flash. 'Build d-bot,'
Hunter said aloud. He tapped
the button. A new image
popped up.

Then the voice began counting
down. '**100, 99, 98, 97...**'

Oh, no! Hunter thought. *That's
not much time to make a d-bot
that can catch a flying dino!*

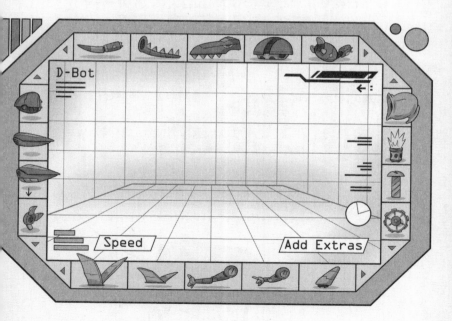

But Hunter knew a lot about dinosaurs. He thought about the dino he needed to catch. Then he began to think about how he could catch it.

Pterodactyls roamed the sky!

• Their name means 'winged finger'.
• Very light — good for flying.
• Wingspan — 3-6 metres.
• Slow on land.

ptero

'I have a plan!' Hunter cried.
'Now, how to make the bot
I need. Hmmm.'

'**65, 64, 63, 62...**' the voice
counted down.

Hunter frowned at the screen.
'**Shhhh**, I can't think when there's
noise around me. I hate noise.'

The voice kept counting.
'**55, 54, 53...**'

'**Uurgh!** I've wasted half my time thinking,' Hunter groaned. 'And talking to a dumb touch screen! I have to get to work.'

My d-bot needs to be light, Hunter thought, as he began to build it.

It needs bigger wings than the dino I need to catch.

Light body + big wings = fast.

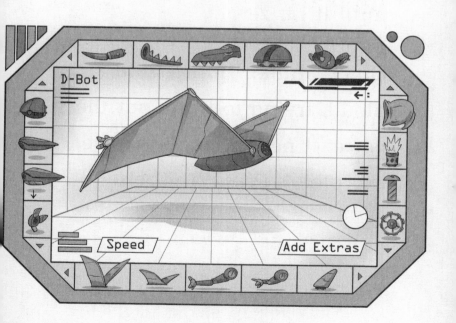

The voice kept counting.
'*29, 28, 27...*' It would not stop
until it hit zero.

'Quick, think!' Hunter said
aloud, trying to block out the
voice. 'I need a hood to cover
the ptero's eyes. What else?'

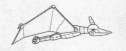

The counting was getting louder.
'**19, 18, 17, 16...**'

'What else, what else?' Hunter
cried, running his hands
through his hair. 'I don't have
much time left. Ah! My bot
needs long legs, so that it can
run fast on land!'

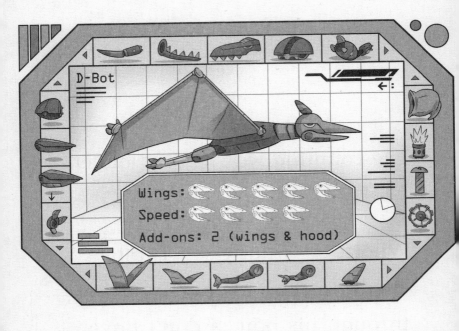

'**10, 9, 8, 7, 6,**' the voice said.
'**Head gear on.**'

'**Aaargh**!' cried Hunter as he grabbed the head gear from the table. 'I'm not sure I'm done!'

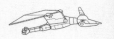

'**5, 4, 3, 2, 1, 0.**' The screen flashed green.

Remote Ready..▮

GAME ON!

Chapter Four

Hunter could not believe what he was seeing. With the head gear on, it was as if he were in another land. A land from long, long ago. There were no cars, no people and no buildings. And Hunter was flying!

All Hunter could see were trees, grass and sky – and a ptero! It was the dino he needed to catch.

I'm back when dinos lived and ruled the land and the sky! thought Hunter. *And I'm flying on my d-bot, high above the trees. This game is cool!*

'*85, 84, 83...*' the voice counted out.

'Oh, no!' Hunter cried. 'Not the timer again. I need to catch this thing fast, with the awesome d-bot I built.'

Hunter could see the dino just ahead. He hit the speed button on his remote. The d-bot picked up speed.

Yes! These wings can really move, thought Hunter. *Go me! Now to fly over the dino and drop the hood over its eyes.*

Hunter got so close that he could have touched the ptero's crest. *I'm almost there,* he thought. He held the speed button down hard on the remote.

One beady eye turned and looked at Hunter. Then, without warning, the ptero dropped from the sky. It flew into a small gap between two walls of rock.

'*35, 34, 33, 32...*' the voice counted.

'I *will* get you,' Hunter said to the ptero. 'You knew my wings wouldn't fit between the walls. But I'm smarter than you.'

Hunter pushed another button on his remote. His d-bot's wings went up. Hunter flew down through the walls of rock after the ptero.

'You're not getting away that easily,' Hunter cried as he gained on the ptero. 'Almost time to drop that hood on you!'

The voice became louder.
'**20, 19, 18...**' Hunter was
running out of time. Again!

He hit the button to let the
hood go.

Hood dropped

As the hood fell over the ptero's
head, it dropped its speed. Then
it began to screech and struggle.
'Screeeek!'

'Now that you can't see where
to fly, you will land,' Hunter
said. He followed the ptero
to the ground. 'And you can't
move very fast on the ground.'

With just fifteen seconds to go,
the ptero flew out from the
walls of rock. It hit the ground.
Then it ran into the trees ahead.

But the ptero was no match for
Hunter's d-bot. Hunter quickly
closed in. He landed his bot
gently onto the ptero's back.

Hunter pushed the button to lower his d-bot's large robotic wings. As the wings wrapped safely around the ptero, it stopped moving.

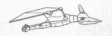

'Gotcha!' cried Hunter, and then he heard the game's voice.

GAME OVER

Hunter wins.
Six seconds left.

Chapter Five

'Well done, Hunter! You passed the test. I knew you would.'

Hunter spun around and took off his head gear. It was Ms Stegg.

'Ms Stegg!' said Hunter. What are you doing here? What am *I* doing here?'

'You're at D-Bot Squad's base,' said Ms Stegg.

'What's D-Bot Squad?' asked Hunter.

Ms Stegg smiled. 'It's a special team that catches dinosaurs.'

'Oh,' said Hunter. 'A special team that gets to play this game. Cool!'

'Well...no. The game was a test,' said Ms Stegg. 'A test to see if you're good enough to catch real dinosaurs. Dinosaurs that are in our world. Right now! Today!'

Hunter gasped. 'So dinosaurs do exist now?' he cried. 'I was right?'

'Yes,' said Ms Stegg. 'You were right, Hunter. Now, screens down.'

Hunter spun around and around, watching as the room's walls filled with screens.

'What are all these?' Hunter
asked, staring at the screens.

'Part of our top-secret work,'
said Ms Stegg. 'And you're
about to join our team. Our
group, Dino Corp, found a way
to bring dinosaurs back to life,
Hunter. Just as they were all
those years ago.'

'**That's awesome!**' cried
Hunter.

'Yes,' said Ms Stegg. 'I'm the
head of Dino Corp. We want to
learn as much as we can from
our dinosaurs. We keep them in
a secret place no one else knows
about.'

'I can't tell anyone about this, then?' Hunter asked.

'That's right. No one must know,' said Ms Stegg.

'And what does D-Bot Squad **do** for Dino Corp?' asked Hunter.

'Well,' Ms Stegg began, 'we must keep the dinosaurs safe. The problem is that a few escaped.

'D-Bot Squad's job is to catch them before anyone sees them.'

'But how will you ever find them again?' asked Hunter.

'That's the easy part,' said Ms Stegg. 'Each dinosaur has a tag. It helps us find them.'

'What's the hard part?' asked Hunter.

'The hard part is catching them,' said Ms Stegg. 'We can only do this with dinosaur-robots, d-bots. That's why we need people like you in D-Bot Squad, Hunter. People who know a lot about dinosaurs and can build really good dinosaur robots.'

'I can do that!' said Hunter.

'Yes, you built the best d-bot to catch that pterodactyl. And you did it really fast!'

Hunter felt proud. What would the super-hero kids think now?

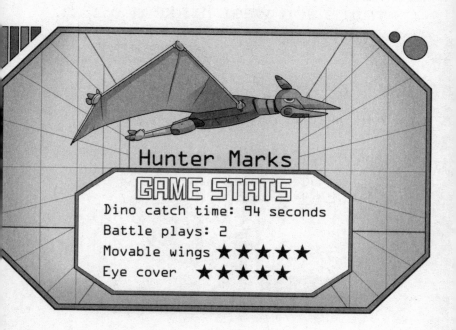

Hunter Marks

GAME STATS

Dino catch time: 94 seconds
Battle plays: 2
Movable wings ★★★★★
Eye cover ★★★★★

Hunter wanted to know more. 'What happens once you catch the dinosaurs?' he asked.

'Well, then we use the d-band,' said Ms Stegg. 'Here, this one's yours. You wear it like a watch.'

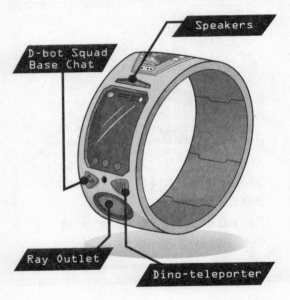

Speakers

D-bot Squad
Base Chat

Ray Outlet

Dino-teleporter

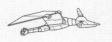

'The d-band teleports the dinosaurs back to the safe place,' Ms Stegg went on.

'Woah!' said Hunter. 'I'll be able to do *that* with this d-band?'

'Yes,' said Ms Stegg. 'Once we've shown you how to use it. First, you need to change into your D-Bot Squad gear.'

Ms Stegg opened a door to a little change room. Hunter went inside. There was a uniform hanging on a hook. There was also a helmet and cool-looking tool belt on a chair. Hunter could not wait to put it all on.

He changed quickly and went
back out to Ms Stegg.

'Good!' she said. 'The uniform is
a perfect fit. You look great!'

Hunter thought so too.

'Now, your d-band has two
buttons,' Ms Stegg added.
'The first button lets you talk
to me.

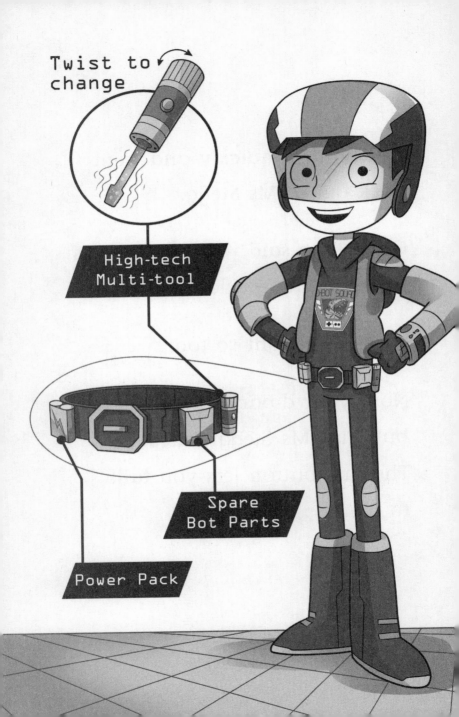

Twist to change

High-tech Multi-tool

Spare Bot Parts

Power Pack

'The second button will teleport the dinosaur to our safe place. The tool belt is for fixing and working on your d-bot.'

'Do you mean the d-bot I built in the game?' Hunter asked.

Ms Stegg smiled. 'That's exactly what I mean.'

'Stand back,' warned Ms Stegg. 'Here it comes.'

Hunter watched as a part of the floor slid open. Then up rose the d-bot that he had built in the game.

'It's mine!' Hunter gasped, running over to it.

'Climb on, Hunter,' Ms Stegg urged. 'There's no time to lose. That pterodactyl you saw through the window was real. You must catch it – **fast!**'

I'm really going to fly a d-bot, Hunter thought. *And I'm going to catch a real ptero!*

Chapter Six

Hunter climbed onto his d-bot.
He leant forward over its neck.
He took a remote from a slot
on the bot's neck. 'It's just like
the remote from the game,' he
said. 'This will be easy!'

'Riding a d-bot for real isn't as easy as in the game,' Ms Stegg warned. 'Go slowly at first, until you get the hang of it.'

Hunter smiled. 'I can do this, Ms Stegg,' he said. 'I'll get that ptero for you.'

'Good luck, Hunter,' Ms Stegg said, stepping away from the d-bot.

'And remember,' Ms Stegg went on, 'press that first d-band button if you need me.'

Hunter put his helmet on. He hit his d-bot's start button and then tapped its speed button.

The roof above him opened. His d-bot's jets fired up. Then his d-bot shot up through the roof like a rocket.

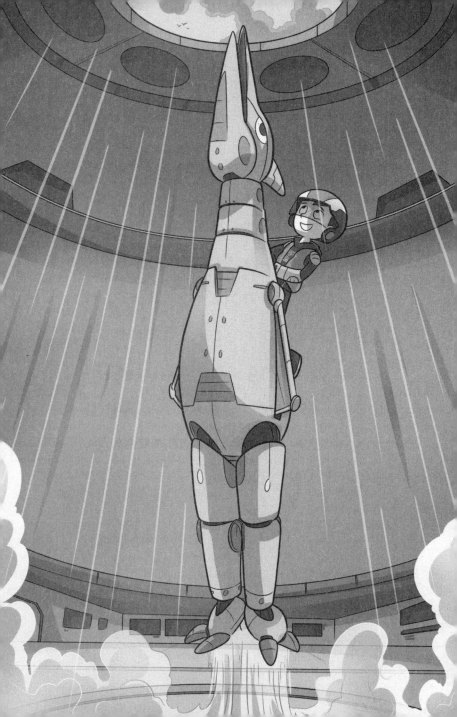

The bot's wings popped out from its body. They flapped hard and fast. Hunter bounced up and down. Wind rushed into his face, pushing at him. Hunter let go of the remote. It hung from the d-bot by its cord.

Hunter wrapped both arms around his d-bot's neck. *It's going too fast and climbing too high*, he thought. *And it's so bumpy!*

He tried to reach the remote. As he did, he slipped. **'Oh no!'** he cried out. 'I'm going to fall off!'

Will Hunter be able

to catch the ptero?

Read Book 2, *Sky High*,

to find out...